This could be our . . .

LAST CHANCE

And sometimes we only get one last chance!

LAST CHANCE

When the Fate of Mankind Collides
with Two Bungling Dice Dealers on
Vacation in the Alaskan Wilderness

DAVID CREPS

Last Chance
When the Fate of Mankind Collides with Two Bungling Dice
Dealers on Vacation in Alaska

Published by Boogie Woogie Books and David Creps
ISBN: 978-1-7354725-2-2

This book–which may hold the key to preventing the human species from continuing down its current, rapid, and obvious path to everlasting extinction–is dedicated to the reaction that I expect to hear from Steven Spielberg upon his learning that he has been chosen to produce and direct the movie version of this story:

"Oh my God!!! Thank you, David!! Thank you!!"

CHAPTER ONE

Imagine this: 1999. In black and white, a globe of the world slowly revolves. Pinpoints of light appear on it in relation to the accented voice of the various newscasters delivering the day's news.

A middle-eastern voice speaks, "Two rival terrorist groups, *The Sword of God's Law* and its main rival The Fist of Heavenly Righteousness, are both claiming responsibility for a bomb which exploded in a crowded Baghdad marketplace killing thirty shoppers. Many more were maimed and injured in this most recent–"

A pinpoint of light illuminates Baghdad.

A Russian voice is now heard, "Forty-seven Russian teenagers participating in a musical celebration of Fyodor Tchaikovsky's life were killed today when Chechen rebels surrounded a concert hall and opened fire–"

A pinpoint of light illuminates Moscow.

As the Russian voice trails off, a Columbian voice is heard, "In a vicious display of wanton violence, the school attended by the son of drug lord Pedro Morales was attacked by members of a newly formed cartel intent on controlling the worldwide flow of cocaine.

"Thirty-seven children are believed dead–"

A pinpoint of light illuminates Bogota.

An African voice is then heard, "In one of the worst outbreaks of violence in recent days, a gang of machete-wielding soldiers rampaged through a refugee camp on the Liberian coast butchering scores of women and children, and throwing their bodies into the River of Sacred Hope."

A pinpoint of light illuminates Monrovia.

The voice of an American network anchorman now delivers the evening news, "In America, new statistics just released by the President's Council on Violence shows a fourteen percent jump in violent crime committed by children under the age of ten, another clear indication that as the problem continues to worsen. No one seems to know what to do about it."

A pinpoint of light illuminates Washington, D.C.

The revolving globe recedes, and as it grows smaller and smaller, it becomes brighter and brighter with pinpoints of light, until finally, it is just one tiny bulb of solid light.

CHAPTER TWO

It is autumn in a picturesque English countryside. A heavy iron gate with a guard post secures a long meandering entranceway leading down to a grand estate.

In the scientific laboratory inside the estate, twenty to thirty scientists in white smocks give their attention to an old, white-haired man who stands in front of a chalkboard that is covered with complicated equations. "And so, gentlemen, I am tremendously pleased to tell you that these last three years of twelve-hour workdays, devoid of the normal comforts and pleasures that one derives from home and family . . . have finally born the fruit which we have all dreamed might be possible within our lifetime."

Removing his glasses, the old man continues, "Gentlemen, tonight I proudly announce to you that the search for a genetically engineered formula which will eliminate all violent tendencies from the human nature . . . has, been, successful."

The scientists react with emotional cries of "Hear, hear," "Thank God," etc. The old man smiles and continues, "And though we still need another year or so to cross-check all your contributing data, and to establish the conditions under which we shall implement the worldwide distribution of our discovery . . . the thing is, as they say in America, 'a done deal.'"

He moves closer to the scientists and continues, "Congratulations on behalf of all mankind. You have accomplished nothing less than the preservation of the human species."

He puts his glasses back on. "Please take the weekend off, go home, enjoy your families, and I will see you back in the labs on Monday morning." As the scientists move to leave, the old man adds one last comment, "And gentlemen, though you may be tempted, in a weak moment, to tell a wife, or a friend–just remember your oath of silence, and consider once again the horrific consequences of this discovery ever getting into the wrong hands. Gentlemen, enjoy your weekend."

The scientists, congratulating each other, exit the laboratory. As the group moves down the hallway, two of the scientists discuss 'the project.'

"Now that we've actually discovered the means for doing it, I'm just not thoroughly convinced we should do it. Do you not have a problem with it?" the first one asks. "Morally, or ethically?"

The other scientist ponders the question. "Well, religion hasn't worked. Politics hasn't worked. And military power hasn't worked. Furthermore, it's my opinion that our days are numbered and that every day that goes by without a solution brings us another day closer to extinction. So, I'm just thankful that science has found a way for the human species to survive. As far as I'm concerned, all the rest of our problems are just trivial shit. You've got to survive before you can evolve."

Another one of the scientists peels away from the group and enters a private office. He closes the door behind him, crosses the room, sits at a desk, and picks up the phone, "I would like to place a call to the United States, please."

CHAPTER THREE

Inside a church rectory, Clayton Sharp sits at a large marble-topped desk surrounded by exquisite hand-woven tapestries, bookcases filled with priceless leather-bound first-edition books, and a gold-framed wall-hanging that reads: "JESUS SAVES–SHARP INVESTS." A phone rings, and he answers, "Reverend Sharp."

Even a brief perusal of the reverend's office would reveal that, for a man of the cloth, the reverend seems to enjoy an ungodly commitment to the fruits of his labor, which, on occasion, has surely inspired various parishioners to wonder, "Who pays for all this stuff?"

The reverend responds to the caller, "Are we talking cash?"

Sharp pauses while the caller replies, and then he dictates his terms: "No bill larger than a hundred. Get me the customs documents that I'll need. Leave the space open for the photo I.D. I'll take care of that myself. Also, forget about meeting anywhere in the Middle East. I'll pick a spot and call you back. And Tommy . . . don't bring the fuckin' donkey with you. Because the next time I see him is gonna be the day he dies. And I'd appreciate it if you give him that message for me."

The reverend hangs up the phone, ponders briefly, opens a telephone book to the yellow pages, jots down a number, and makes a phone call: "Hello, this is Chad Mathews calling for the Reno Gazette-Journal. How are you today? The reason I'm calling is because I'm doing a piece on interesting people who take unusual vacations. And I thought a travel agency with the name–" He pauses a moment, checking the yellow page. "Exotic Adventures, might be a good place to begin my research.

"And what I would like to do is feature someone who is about to leave for some remote area where he will be totally out of contact with civilization.

"Would you have anyone whose exotic vacation might fit that description?"

He pauses to listen before continuing, "Wonderful, ten days without contact with the outside world. And where exactly is it they're going?" He listens, nodding along, and then repeats what he's been told, "Two miles north of Last Chance, Alaska, on the shore of a beautiful lake, isolated deep in the middle of nowhere, which has a small island, inhabited by the only human within a thousand miles." Clayton Sharp leans back in his chair. "Wow. And could I get the correct spelling of your client's name?" He listens again and then repeats the spelling, "H. O. P. P. Y. Is that like hippity-hop . . . Hoppy?"

CHAPTER FOUR

Inside Reno's premiere casino, dealers in black pants, white shirts, black bow ties, black aprons, and black vests embroidered with sparkling gold sequins ascend and descend an escalator.

Bernard L. Latrell, a short, rotund man who might have passed for a "double" of Danny DeVito, steps onto the descending side. He wears oversized pieces of chunky gold jewelry and has his nose buried in the *Sporting News*.

At the bottom of the escalator, a man in his mid-forties, Hoppy Johnson, steps onto the ascending stairs. He has urgent news for Bernard and speaks rapidly as they pass each other, "I gotta tell you something important. Wait for me at the bottom." Hoppy reaches the top and u-turns, stepping onto the descending stairs.

Bernard unwraps a piece of gum and waits for Hoppy at the bottom.

Hoppy guides Bernard off to the side. "I just heard from the Big Dog. He told me to give you a message. He said the next time he hears that you've hustled a bet, you're out the door."

Bernard scoffs. "Aw, bullshit. He ain't gonna fire me. Who's he kidding?"

Bending the gum into his mouth, Bernard heads off to rejoin the other dealers returning to the 'pit' after their break.

Hoppy steps back onto the ascending stairs and makes one last effort to reason with his departing friend, "And he also said he'd better not catch you with gum in your mouth."

Bernard continues into the pit, places his newspaper in a slot inside the podium, then walks over to the dice table to replace the dealer whose turn it is for a break. He has entered a busy dice game. Four different colors of chips are stacked in various heights all across the green-felt layout.

Freddie, the stickman, calls the dice as a brief feel for the game is established. "Eight. Hard."

The dealers lean forward to pick up all the "field bets."

Freddie takes down all the "prop-bets" directly in front of him while wise-cracking to the players in regard to the previous roll of the dice. "Two fours. The ol' ma and pa roll. A pair of squares."

Two young ladies, who are observing the game and standing just outside the half-circle of players making bets, chuckle at Freddie's witty remark.

Freddie winks at them.

Bernard is busy at his end of the table, 'taking, paying, and placing' as he 'hustles.'

In a low voice, as he moves the players' money around, Bernard attempts to get a particular player, Marty (a well-dressed man in his sixties), to make a bet for the dealers. "Hey, Marty, stop. Don't do it."

Bernard turns away from Marty and directs himself to the stickman. "Hey Freddie, did you see that? Did you see what Marty's hand was almost doin'? Marty's hand was almost starting to make a bet for us!"

Freddie now does his part. "No, Marty, no."

The third dealer glances around to make sure neither a pit supervisor nor the shift manager is within hearing distance.

Things are all clear, and the third dealer calls across to the other end of the table. "Don't do it, Marty! Think of your record!"

Marty looks pissed, as though all eyes have been directed to accuse him of being a cheap bastard. Sufficiently coerced, Marty reluctantly takes a chip from the very, very full rack of winnings in front of him and flips it onto the layout.

Bernard picks it up and pitches it over to the stickman. "Boys on eleven, courtesy of Mr. M."

Freddie takes the chip and places it on eleven.

Now, as the dice are about to roll, Bernard begins his next hustle, "Thank you for the bet, Mr. M. You're doing the Lord's work." He then directs himself to all the other players at Marty's end of the table. "He sets a fine example, doesn't he?"

Now, also feeling coerced, intimidated, and shamed, the other players grumble and pitch in a bet-for-the-dealers. "For the boys."

The stickman places the bets on eleven. "The boys thank you. We're gonna go right here on eleven because I'm gonna call it." Freddie then pushes the dice out to the shooter. "All right, shooter, it's eleven time!"

The shooter picks up the dice, shakes them into a melodious rattle, and let's them fly. The dice hit, bounce, and tumble to a stop.

Freddie calls them. "Four! Four! The hard way! Two-dee-two! Well, it wasn't eleven this time, but you can always bet it again. Don't be a quitter."

The dealers then immediately begin the process of dice dealing all over again: take, pay, place . . . hustle.

CHAPTER FIVE

Reverend Clayton leaves his office, walks down a hallway to a narrow staircase, and climbs up to the choir's balcony. There, Tiffany, a highly attractive woman in her early forties, practices a hymn on the huge, open-pipe organ.

She is aware of the reverend but continues playing without acknowledging his presence.

He sits on the rail overlooking an ornate expanse of the church-settings below, with the pews, altar, pulpit, stained-glass windows, and statues all adding a feeling of sanctity while he watches the woman practice.

She finishes, and Clayton speaks, "You play that piece so beautifully. Will you be playing it at tomorrow's service?"

Tiffany, ignoring his question, seems frozen in thought. She takes her time choosing her words, and then still without turning to face him, speaks, "I want it to end."

The reverend leaves the rail and takes up a position against the end of the organ.

She waits for him to say something.

Before long, he smiles. "No, you don't."

Tiffany stands and looks at him. "Yes, I do."

The reverend moves closer. "No, you don't."

Tiffany insists, "Yes, I do."

Taking hold of her shoulders, the reverend eases her slowly backward. As he speaks, her buttocks press against the organ keys, and a loud honking sound from the huge pipes breaks aggressively into the church's otherwise reverent silence. "No, you don't."

Tiffany is determined. "Yes, I do."

Again, accompanied by the loud discordant honk, the reverend is also determined, and replies with a smile, "No, you don't."

She smiles back, "*Yes*, I do."

Again, the honk accompanies the reverend's words. "*No*, you don't."

Downstairs in the church vestibule is a huge stained-glass window depicting Jesus Christ suffering on the cross. As the rising sun shines through the stained glass, the room grows gradually brighter and the intrusive bursts of honking come at shorter and shorter intervals, until there is one thunderous orgasmic final honk.

CHAPTER SIX

Meanwhile, back at the casino, the 'Big Dog' sits at his desk. Bernard stands in front of him.

The Big Dog speaks, "So, let's see if I heard you correctly. You are totally innocent of hustling bets, or chewing gum on the game?"

Bernard answers back, "That is correct. As a matter of fact, I'm the victim here."

The Big Dog raises his eyebrows. "You're the victim?"

Bernard offers a new angle on the situation: "That's right. I'm the one who has been falsely accused here. I'm a victim of the false-accusation syndrome. And, I might add, this is a very serious syndrome. Very serious. Juries have been known to award thousands upon thousands of dollars in punitive damages to victims of this particular syndrome."

The Big Dog leans back in his chair. "Well, let me tell you the reason why I tend to believe you might have been hustling. Dr. Martin Benson just left this office. He came to inform me that he is sending a letter of complaint to the Chairman of the Board and to all major stockholders of the El Dorado Hotel-Casino. And the complaint is going to read something like, 'I've been coming to the El Dorado at least four times a year for the past twenty years, but I'm now considering taking my business to one of the casinos down the street, et cetera, et cetera.'"

He puts his hands behind his head and concludes by saying, "And all this because some asshole dice dealer won't quit hustling him for a bet."

Bernard is offended. "He didn't say it was me, did he?"

The Big Dog seems to almost be enjoying himself. "No, he didn't exactly identify you by name. He seemed a little intimidated. However, I did get the distinct impression that it was you."

"Why, what did he say? That the hustler was a good-looking dude with a cool personality?"

"Not exactly. I believe his words were, 'a wise-ass shrimp with a big fuckin' mouth.'"

Bernard takes the insult in stride. "So, how do I figure into it?"

"You chewing gum?"

"No."

"You're not chewing gum?"

"No."

"What is it you're chewing?"

"Nothing. Just air."

"Open your mouth."

Bernard swallows noticeably, presumably ridding his mouth of the gum, then he 'opens wide'.

Big Dog raises the stakes. "When do you start your vacation?"

Bernard smiles. "Tomorrow."

"Do me a favor while you're on vacation."

"Sure, what do you need?"

"I'd like you to spend some time considering what other casino you might like to work at. Maybe you'd like to go to the Peppermill, or the Silver Legacy. Tokes are good, both places."

Bernard responds as he stands to leave, "Naw. I like it here. I like working for you. Sometimes, you're a little uptight, but most of the time, you're pretty darn easy to get along with." On his way out the door, he pauses for a brief exchange, "Is this ass-chewing over?"

The Big Dog spells things out for him. "I'm gonna catch you myself, Latrell. And when I do . . . you're out the door."

Bernard now spells things out for the Big Dog, "Okay. Just don't forget to have your lawyers put the 'L' in my name when they're writing out the check. Bernard L. Latrell." He then gives the Big Dog a friendly thumbs-up and strolls off down the hallway.

* * *

Bernard and Hoppy have just gotten off work and are now in the dealer's locker-room, putting their bow ties, aprons, and vests into their lockers.

Written with a black magic-marker on white adhesive tape, the large letters over Hoppy's locker spell: HOPPY JOHNSON.

Hoppy lowers his voice to confide with Bernard. "So, just make sure you don't tell anybody, okay?"

Bernard, preoccupied with getting to the bar, swings his locker door shut, twists the combination lock, and heads for the urinals. "Yeah, yeah."

Hoppy follows him, stands at an adjacent urinal, and pees along with Bernard as he emphasizes his request. "Really. Don't even tell one person, or you'll ruin everything."

Bernard is mildly curious. "Why is that?"

Again Hoppy emphasizes the importance of his request: "*Because*, the point is to get out and away from everybody. And if anybody knows where we are, then it's not the same thing."

Bernard checks his bald-spot and reconfigures a few strands. "Why is that?"

Hoppy attempts to reason it out, gesturing as he talks. "Because! Don't you see? We're gonna be out there surviving on just our wits. We don't want any 'backup.' We want to be out there working without a net."

Bernard has a few concerns of his own. "What if we need to be rescued?"

"We'll do it ourselves!" Hoppy says reassuringly.

"We'll rescue ourselves? I never heard of that. I don't think people are supposed to rescue themselves. I think people are supposed to get rescued by other people."

"Bernard, please, I'm begging you, don't tell one single person where we're going. Okay?"

Bernard zips up his pants, hits the flushing lever, then moves to a row of washbasins where he can look in the mirror, wash his hands, and re-comb his bald spot. "Yeah, yeah."

* * *

Bernard and Hoppy leave the locker room and head for the employee's bar for the traditional after-shift drink.

They snake their way through the crowd, with Bernard slowing down only long enough to make a few sarcastic comments to the stickman seen earlier on the dice game. "Nice hustling, Freddie. How much you add to the pot today, twenty cents?"

Freddie defends himself, "Hey Bernard, maybe you didn't hear, the Big Dog says the hustling is history."

Bernard puts an edge on his response, "But you did take your share of the pie today, didn't you?"

Freddie takes the bait. "Hey, asshole, I do my part. I put in my share."

Bernard can't stop shaming Freddie. "You do? I never noticed that."

Freddie stands his ground. "You got amnesia? You don't remember the day I got us the thousand-dollar chip?"

"Yeah. The asshole wins a hundred and eighty grand and throws us one chip on his way to cash out. And all because you say, 'Thanks for playing.'"

Bernard sneers. "Nice fuckin' job, Freddie. Nice hustle. Nice the way you didn't put too much pressure on him."

Freddie is on his heels. "Yeah, well, I didn't see you refuse to take your cut of it, did I?"

Bernard now uses the bottom-line reality that all dice dealers understand. "You're right. I did take my two hundred and fifty-dollar cut. But you know what, when I was folding that two hundred and fifty bucks into my wallet, I couldn't help but wonder what my cut would have been if the asshole had landed on my end of the game.

"Whaddya think, five, ten grand, minimum? Whaddya think ol' Bernard would have pulled into the pot if the asshole had been on my end of the game–where I could have come in close and gotten personal."

Freddie mumbles some inadequate face-saving comment as Bernard turns away and motions to get the bartender's attention.

The bartender spots Bernard and re-wipes the already-clean area in front of the *Reserved* sign in the middle of the bar where Bernard takes his seat.

Hoppy gets comfortable, standing with one foot on the bottom rung of Bernard's stool.

The bartender removes the sign and, without waiting to be told, immediately delivers a martini and a glass of beer.

Hoppy takes the beer and lays a ten-dollar bill onto the bar.

Bernard picks the olive out of the martini, savors it, and takes a sip. He then peels a twenty off of his bankroll, slides it across the bar, and critiques the martini. "Perfectimondo."

With a smile, the bartender picks up the twenty and the ten. And before moving off to the register to ring up the drinks and pocket his thirteen dollars worth of tips, he re-affirms his servitude. "Exactly as you ordered, Mr. B."

Bernard turns his attention to Hoppy. "Maybe we ought to celebrate tonight. Maybe the occasion calls for a little trip out to the Pussycat Ranch. Whaddya say?"

Hoppy finishes his beer and sets the empty glass on the bar. "I don't think so."

Bernard scoffs. "Why, you gotta rush home to see some P.B.S. documentary about endangered bullfrogs on the Kalahari?"

Hoppy smiles, "Tonight, I'm gonna re-sharpen my Swiss Army knife, repack my backpack, and get some sleep."

Bernard gives him a look. "Yeah, that's a good idea, that sounds like a lot of fun. I might do that myself. Or, I might just get drunk and go to the cat house." He drains his martini. "It's kind of a 'toss-up.'"

Hoppy laughs and turns to leave. "See you at five o'clock. Be listening for my honk." He then gives Bernard a strange little 'goodbye wave' by flicking two of his fingers up and down, rapidly, five or six times under his chin.

Bernard reacts. "Yeah, okay, see ya."

The bartender, having observed Hoppy's finger-waving exit, approaches Bernard. "Mr. B., can I ask you something?"

Bernard answers, "As long as it ain't about art, politics, or religion."

The bartender nods then asks, "Every night when Hoppy leaves, he does this to you." He imitates Hoppy's finger-wave. "Why?"

Bernard responds, "You don't want to know. It's a . . . Webelo thing." He then pulls a cigar out of his breast pocket. "Trust me, you don't want to know."

"Is it a gang thing?"

Bernard chuckles, "Naw, I don't think you'd call the Webelos a gang. They're more like . . . an organization."

With a slight gesture toward his empty glass, Bernard makes his wishes known.

The bartender responds immediately and returns with a fresh martini and a light for Bernard's cigar.

Laying another twenty onto the bar, Bernard speaks to him in a confidential tone, "Raymond, did you know that I am leaving at five o'clock tomorrow morning to spend ten days in the wilderness exactly two miles north of Last Chance, Alaska?"

* * *

Leaving the bar, Hoppy emerges through the employee's entrance/exit and walks down the street to the corner where he joins a group of five old men–conventioneers from 'Back East,' all in their seventies or eighties, all wearing old, weathered, 'Baltimore Colts' jackets, all waiting for the light to change.

Before the green walk-light comes on, Hoppy offers them a little hometown friendliness. "You guys must be Colts fans from way back."

Like all old guys who don't want to engage in pointless conversation, the old men grunt their responses without encouraging any further discussion.

But Hoppy likes old guys. "My dad used to be a big Colts fan. He used to tell me about when they were the best team in the world. When they had Johnny Unitas and Raymond Berry. And Big Daddy Lipscombe. And Alan 'The Horse' Ameche. And Lenny Moore. And Donovan."

The old guys brighten in response to the utterance of these revered names.

Having gotten their attention, Hoppy continues, "I met Johnny Unitas once. At a Boy Scout banquet. He shook my hand. But ya know, the thing I remember most about the Colts was that Championship game back in '69, when they played the Jets. Remember that one? What a game. I was only a kid, but I'll never forget it." He exhales in sadness. "Who would have ever thought the Baltimore Colts would get their butts kicked by the lowly New York Jets."

The old guys become instantaneously apoplectic, gasping for air.

The light changes to green, and Hoppy heads off, waving over his shoulder as he leaves. "Have a nice day."

The old guys are wheezing and coughing, trying to recover from the sudden memory of 'that game.'

One of them has had his knees buckle under him and is being attended to by another one who is doing his best to minimize the shock. Another, who has a cane, is endeavored in a futile attempt to catch up with Hoppy and whack him over the head.

Another is attempting to restrain 'the caner,' "Easy, Jimmy. Easy."

And another adds moral support to his fallen comrade. "He's a lying sack of shit. He never met Johnny U."

* * *

Hoppy drives his old, beat-up pickup truck off a quiet desert highway and heads for the small isolated mobile home in the distance.

He pulls up and gets out, and just as he is about to enter the trailer, Tiffany steps out of the shadows and smiles. "Hoppy Johnson?"

Hoppy reacts with a startled friendliness. "Yes, ma'am."

At this point, a baton to the back of Hoppy's head renders him unconscious, and he falls back into the Reverend Clayton's arms.

Clayton lays him out flat on the ground. He then notices Tiffany's hesitance. "Come on, hurry up, he won't be out very long. Find me that driver's license."

Tiffany still seems reluctant. "Are you sure we're doing the right thing?"

"Honey, right now, we don't have time to discuss it. You'll have to just trust me on this."

"You're absolutely certain that we should be doing this?"

"Just trust me."

Tiffany takes the wallet out of Hoppy's back pocket and, while Clayton prepares a long hypodermic needle, searches it for Hoppy's driver's license. The reverend inserts the needle into Hoppy's arm and draws out a full syringe of blood, which he then caps and places securely into a briefcase. With everything completed, he motions Tiffany into the car, and off they go with the blood and the driver's license.

CHAPTER SEVEN

At the Reno-Lake Tahoe International Airport, Hoppy and Bernard approach the United Airlines check-in counter.

Their plane is soon to take off.

Hoppy and Bernard sit next to each other. Bernard is in the throes of a monstrous hangover. Hoppy gingerly touches the sore spot on his head. "I don't know what happened. I think I was mugged by a girl."

"Too bad she didn't steal your watch."

"Hey, my Uncle Mort gave me this watch on the day I graduated from Cub Scouts and became a Webelo. He was trying to make up with me."

"Hoppy, let me ask you something. What exactly is a Webelo?"

"Well, after you finish Cub Scouts, before you start Boy Scouts, you become a Webelo."

"Yeah, so what the hell is it?"

"It's the thing you are between Cub Scouts and Boy Scouts."

"I know that! You already told me that! What I want to know is what 'is' a Webelo! It's something; what the fuck is it?!"

"I dunno."

Bernard clinches his teeth in exasperation, turns away from Hoppy, slaps his pillow into shape, and clears his mind before closing his eyes. "Do not talk to me again before we get to Alaska. And by the way, if watches hadn't been invented yet, and your watch was the only watch in the world, I still wouldn't be caught dead wearing it."

* * *

Hours later, at the airport in Anchorage, Alaska, Hoppy and Bernard pass through the security checkpoint.

They then climb into a small Cessna with pontoons and the words "GRIZZLY BEAR AIRLINES" painted on its side.

Soon, they are directly above an isolated lake deep within this astonishingly beautiful wilderness, and the Cessna begins its descent. Hoppy stares out the window, sharing his thoughts, "Look out there. This wilderness–it's so beautiful, so clean, so primitive, so perfect. Sometimes, I feel that things back home are just too complicated to ever figure out. I wish everything was the way it used to be when everybody was tuned into the same things. I sure miss the 50s, don't you?"

Bernard scoffs at the thought of it. "What the hell are you talking about? I wasn't around in the 50s. Neither were you."

"I know, but I've heard my parents talk about it, and it really sounded great."

"Aw, bullshit. The whole thing was overrated. They didn't even have color TV in the 50s."

"Yeah, but they had neighborhoods where everybody knew everybody else."

Bernard is not impressed, "So what? Who wants to know the yahoos living next door to you? Who needs that aggravation?"

"But–"

"But nothing! My neighbors live in their house. I live in my house. They don't bother me; I don't bother them. *That* is a perfect neighborhood."

"But in the 50s, people used to talk to each other, face-to-face."

"Why? If you want to hear people talk, turn on the TV."

"I'm not talking about hearing words. I'm talking about conversation. Communication. The enjoyment of discovering the things you have in common with another human being."

Bernard offers Hoppy a different perspective, "Let me tell you something. Last Sunday, I was in my bathroom, taking a dump, and the window was open, and while I'm sitting there, I can hear my neighbors' TV. And do you know what he's watching? Cartoons.

"Can you believe that! Sunday morning, during a 49ers game, and this guy is watching cartoons. Like the Road Runner dropping a bowling ball off a cliff onto a coyote's head is more satisfying than watching the 9ers beat the livin' shit out of Miami."

Bernard breathes deeply. "So, what could this guy and I possibly have in common. Besides, if you start communicating with your neighbors, and then you have a disagreement–they might shoot you. Unless you can shoot them first."

* * *

The plane lands on the lake and taxis up to the shore. Its single propeller stops, and its pilot disembarks to stretch his limbs, followed shortly by Hoppy, who is beside himself with happiness, and Bernard, who looks totally annoyed.

The pilot speaks, "Well, here you are. Except for the guy who lives out there on Last Chance Island," he says, indicating to the island, "there isn't another human within a thousand miles. He's got the telephone if you need it."

Hoppy nods.

The pilot adds, "I want to start back while I still have some daylight, so you boys go ahead and get yourselves unloaded, and I'll be getting outta here."

Hoppy goes to the side of the plane, opens the cargo door, and pulls out a backpack.

Bernard peels two twenties off his bankroll and approaches

the pilot. "I got a bad back, do you think you could unload my stuff for me?"

The pilot responds, "Sorry. I'm the pilot, not the unloader."

Bernard peels another twenty off his bankroll and adds it to his offer. "Here. I'm not kidding; I got a bad back. I couldn't unload that stuff even if I wanted to."

The pilot replies, "Sorry. It's a matter of principle with me." He lights a cigarette. "If a man can't carry his own load, he shouldn't be traveling so heavy."

Bernard sweetens his offer, "Listen to me. I got . . . a bad . . . back. Now, tell me how much it would take for you to unload my stuff! Gimme a number! Seventy bucks, eighty bucks, a hundred–how much?"

The pilot clarifies his position, "Like I just told you, I'm the pilot. Period."

Bernard persists, "One-twenty! One-forty!"

The pilot brings the conversation to a close, "And furthermore, in approximately five minutes, this pilot is gonna take that plane, and with or without all that shit of yours onboard– get the hell out of here." The pilot turns and walks back toward the plane.

Bernard follows close behind. "Thank you! Thank you very much!" He sweeps the air with his arm. "I shall recommend you to all my friends," he says, addressing an imaginary throng of friends, "Grizzly Bear Airlines, where the service is . . . impeccable!"

The pilot pinches out his cigarette, puts the butt into his shirt pocket, climbs into the plane, and closes the door.

Bernard yells to Hoppy as he stomps over to the cargo door. "Excuse me!"

Hoppy responds, "What?"

Bernard answers back, "What? Whaddya think!"

"I like the way the pilot put it, 'If you can't carry it yourself, you shouldn't have it with you.'"

The response pisses Bernard off. "Hey! Get over here and gimme a hand with this shit!"

Hoppy doesn't budge on matters of 'principle.' "Sorry, Bern. It's a matter of principle."

Bernard sucks in a deep breath, lets it out, and reaches into the cargo bay.

As he pulls a large, expensive, battery-powered TV into his arms, he directs a comment to the pilot. "Usually, this is about the time that I start kicking a little ass."

* * *

Under a rising moon, on a picturesque road in the English countryside, Clayton and Tiffany sit in a parked car going over the plan one final time.

The grand estate with the scientific laboratories and an armed security post is just a short distance down the road.

Tiffany is nervous about the plan. "I don't like this."

Clayton attempts to reassure her, "Nothing to worry about. It's a piece of cake. Trust me."

"But what if–"

"There's not going to be a 'what if.' You're gonna walk by, comment to the security guard on it being such a lovely evening for a walk, and distract him with just enough idle conversation to give me time to cross the side-lawn. It'll be a friendly, non-suspicious, brief exchange. And off you go. Then I'll meet you back at the hotel when I'm finished."

Clayton exits the car, then holds Tiffany's door open.

CHAPTER EIGHT

Meanwhile, at a gravelly lake-shore campsite, Bernard eats from a can of pork and beans. He whacks the last blob back into the can, then sets it down and smacks his lips. "That was fabulous! You told me you were one hell of a cook, but I had no idea you could put together a spread like this. Imagine, pork . . . and beans."

Hoppy is at peace with the world. "Hey, relax. We're on vacation. Kick back. Put your feet up."

Bernard is disgusted. "Why did I let you talk me into this? I could have been in Vegas. What time is it?"

Hoppy looks at his wristwatch. "It is exactly ten hundred hours . . . in Honolulu."

"I don't give a shit what time it is in Honolulu! What time is it right here where I'm sitting!"

Hoppy takes another look at his wristwatch. "It is seventeen hundred hours . . . in Bombay."

"That watch doesn't do Alaska time, does it?"

Again, Hoppy checks his watch. "How about Copenhagen?"

"Forget it. It doesn't matter if we know what time it is for the next ten days."

Hoppy agrees. "Yeah, what difference does it make?"

"Oh, no difference. Except maybe in just that one little, minor, little way."

"What way is that?"

"Ya can't go anywhere! Say a Columbo re-run is gonna be on in three and a half hours–how can you go anywhere? How the fuck would you know when it's time to come back?"

Bernard flips the TV Guide into the campfire. He's seated in a recliner, with his amenities close by: a battery-powered television set, a tent, an air mattress, a sleeping bag, a bug lantern, and a custom-made suitcase filled with gin, vermouth, jars of green olives, and many bags of Fritos.

On the television screen, Greg Holt anchors the news. "There is an interesting story coming out of England today. NBC News sources have learned that a highly secret academy of British scientists has made a monumental breakthrough in the field of genetic engineering. By isolating a single gene from one particular chromosome, they have supposedly succeeded in eliminating the capacity for violence within the human nature." Greg shifts the papers on his desk. "However, according to other scientists polled by NBC News, it is felt that any breakthrough in regard to the precise alteration of human behavior is still many years into the future."

He lightens his tone as he continues, "In tonight's other top story, from Hollywood, here's Wendy Hogarth."

"Good evening, America. A two-billion-dollar deal has just been announced by Bob Palmer, the president of the newly created motion picture studio, *Squint and Grunt Productions*."

She smiles. "For their first production, they have attached twelve of Hollywood's biggest, toughest, meanest, and most heterosexual-looking stars to shoot, slash, and stab their way into your hearts, in a wonderful script adapted from the New York Times critically acclaimed number-one best-selling book: *Cool Things to Say When You Are Killing Someone*."

Wendy smiles again. "The film is already being heralded as the most violently sadistic romantic-comedy ever attempted."

She flashes her gorgeous Hollywood smile again. "This is Wendy Hogarth . . . from Hollywood."

Bernard rolls his eyes in disgust. "Shit. Is that all they know how to make anymore . . . chick flicks?"

* * *

Clayton and Tiffany stand on a balcony looking out on London's city lights. They sip champagne. Clayton feels amorous, but Tiffany is still unresolved over matters regarding their relationship.

Clayton moves his face close to hers. "You were wonderful today."

Tiffany turns and looks away. But Clayton pursues. "I couldn't have done it without you."

Tiffany seems a bit defensive. "I'm the only one who could have distracted the guard? A dog couldn't have done it?"

Clayton brings the God-element into the conversation: "I want you to feel good about what we're doing. It's not for us to judge the strange ways in which the Lord works. When we're called, we answer. It's as simple as that."

Tiffany shrugs and turns squarely to Clayton. "And what about us?"

Clayton persists. "*What about us*? We're in London, we have an exceptional bottle of champagne, the night has a few more hours left in it, and all the hard work is finished."

Tiffany remains steadfast. "I mean what about us and children, and a home, and pets, and a garden; the things that will bind us together as we grow older. What about that stuff?"

Clayton, annoyed by her usual preoccupation with the 'family thing,' returns to the champagne bucket for a refill. "I take you to the finest restaurants; I buy you diamond jewelry; I place you on a balcony sipping champagne in the heart of London." He turns to face her. "What is it you want?"

"I want a couple of kids and a chicken farm."

With a quick reactionary slurp, Clayton empties his glass and speaks as he heads for the door, "This is 1999, Tiffany.

You're no longer in your twenties–life goes on. I'll be in the bar if you need me."

Clayton exits with Tiffany shouting after him. "And quit calling me Tiffany! My name is Lulabell!"

CHAPTER NINE

It's daybreak, and Hoppy sits at a campfire, gleefully frying eggs. Loud snoring emanates from Bernard's tent.

Before long, Hoppy calls to Bernard, "Wake up, Mr. B."

The snoring does not cease.

Hoppy tries again, louder. "Hey, Bernard! Wake up! You're gonna miss the sunrise!"

The snoring sputters momentarily but soon returns to full force.

Again, Hoppy tries–even louder. "Hey, Mr. B., look! Naked babes!"

The snoring sputters to a stop. Movement is heard inside the tent. Bernard steps out, glances around, stretches the stiffness out of his back, farts, and moves towards the campfire.

He wears baby-blue, monogrammed, silk pajamas. "Ya

know, last night, as I was lying there in my sleeping bag, on a plastic air mattress, less than six inches off the actual frozen ground, I got to wondering–" He pulls out a cigar. "Why is it that, of all the people who would like to hang around with me, I let you?" He lights the cigar and continues, "Why is that do you suppose?"

Hoppy sees that the eggs are ready to be flipped over, so he makes an attempt. They fly unceremoniously through the air and land flat on the ground. He then addresses Bernard. "I guess we just hang around together because . . . I dunno." He picks up the coffee pot. "God, doesn't it feel good to be alive!"

Bernard ignores the upside-down eggs near his feet and holds out his empty cup. Hoppy pours steaming coffee into the cup, but then accidentally drips a few drops onto Bernard's hand. Bernard shrieks and spills half the cup.

In a measured cadence, Bernard now expresses his pent-up frustration. "That's what I'm talking about. You are an idiot. I am not. So, why in the hell are we hanging around together?"

Hoppy laughs as he cracks four more eggs into the frying pan. "How do you like that coffee?"

Bernard sighs deeply, takes in the surroundings, sighs again, and takes a long sip from his half-empty coffee cup. Then, after a few seconds of savoring, Bernard spews the coffee down the front of his baby blue pajamas as he buckles onto the ground. Thrashing back and forth, Bernard struggles to get over the pain and suffering. At last, he gets himself under control.

And now, fully awake and filthy dirty, he makes his feelings known. "I could sue you for that!"

"You didn't like it, did you?"

With some loud, fast spitting, Bernard attempts to cleanse himself of the last vestiges of Hoppy's coffee.

The spitting continues as Hoppy shares the secret of his recipe. "That was one-part Columbian, mountain-grown, coffee beans, and three-parts Mexican, mountain-grown, chile beans. I invented it."

* * *

Later, after things have settled down, Hoppy struggles to drag fallen logs from the forest to the lakeshore.

Bernard sits in the recliner eating Fritos dipped in guacamole, and watching "trash tv."

The host speaks to his guest, "So, your unemployed husband, who physically beats you regularly, was having affairs with four of your neighbors, in your bed, while you were out working a second job to pay off his gambling debts, correct?"

The guest answers, "Yes."

The host responds, "Well then, I guess my next question is: Why do you stay with him?"

The guest answers with tears in her eyes, "I don't know. I guess because I love him."

"How can you love a man like that?"

"I don't know. I just do."

The host turns to the audience, "Well, unbeknownst to our guest, we have invited her husband to join us here today. So, stay tuned, and when we come back, we'll see what this wife has to say to her husband–the man responsible for turning her into such a disgustingly pitiful creature."

The television suddenly goes blank, and the following words scroll across the screen: "DCT NEWS SPECIAL REPORT."

A broadcaster steps forward to make an announcement, "Good afternoon. We interrupt our regularly scheduled program to bring you a special report from foreign correspondent James Merrills in London, England."

A man with a British accent now takes over. "Thank you. The story here in London unfolds thusly: Sometime between dusk last night and dawn this morning, that secretive academy of scientists, now identified as the British Institute of Genetic Research–the same group of scientists who first cloned sheep from a stem cell–have had their laboratory broken into. And it is rumored that a 'vial' containing a futuristic genetic formula, which is claimed to be capable of altering human behavior–along with another vial containing its only known vaccine–have been stolen.

"At this juncture, I should hasten to add that this has not been officially confirmed. However, authorities do say they are confident the thief will be soon apprehended, as they believe this crime to be the work of an amateur. Sources close to MI5 report there is internal speculation that the thief may be just a clumsy opportunist who apparently cut himself very badly as he entered by breaking through a window. Or possibly, it was a member of some terrorist organization. The one thing we have been able to confirm is that there was a substantial loss of blood at the scene of the crime, and that Scotland Yard has already begun running DNA tests on it.

"We shall keep you periodically informed as this story develops. This is James Merrills from London, England."

The American broadcaster now confirms the importance of the story: "DCT News will keep you updated on this very, very, important story. We now return you to our regular programming."

The host returns to the television screen. The husband and the wife are seated on the stage, side-by-side. The host addresses the wife, "Okay Mrs. Johnson, go ahead, tell this man everything you've ever wanted to tell him. Go ahead, let it all out."

The wife looks at the husband and inhales a long breath of air before speaking. "I'm sorry." She then directs herself to the host. "He couldn't help it; he had a rough childhood."

Bernard chuckles. "Yeah, that's right, it ain't his fault. He's a victim of the crappy-childhood syndrome." He then stands and uses the remote control to turn off the television. Stretching his arms without spilling his martini, he calls over to Hoppy, who is still struggling with the logs, "Hey. What time's lunch?"

Hoppy looks at his wristwatch and answers with a smile, "About fourteen-thirty . . . Barcelona time."

Bernard gives him a look, then sits back in his recliner, stirs his martini, refills his bowl of Fritos, and clicks the television back on.

A political campaign advertisement now appears on the television screen. It features a picture of a sinister-looking man in a suit, with the U.S. Senate Building in the background. A professionally serious voice accompanies the picture, "This is United States Senator Jim Ribbons. Mr. Ribbons is once again running for the U.S. Senate from the state of Alaska. Before you make your choice on election day, there are a few things we think you should know about Jim Ribbons.

"Mr. Ribbons is a swindler, a chiseler, an abuser of women and children, a coward, a thief, a liar, and a shameless nose-picker who wouldn't know the difference between a rainbow trout and a moose turd."

Now, the voice of Ribbon's opposing candidate ends the ad, "This paid political advertisement was brought to you by the *Citizens for Progressive Leadership*, a committee to elect Peter Jones to the United States Senate."

A different paid political ad now comes onto the screen. It's a picture of a short, smiling man with a huge head of hair, in a suit, alongside a cartoonishly designed garbage bin with the word "LOONY" written on its side.

Another professional announcer's voice speaks as the

picture tilts gradually toward the bin, "This man, Peter Jones, is a moron. He is also a pornographer, an adulterer, a crook, a drug dealer, and–under that cheap–stupid-looking wig . . . a bald-headed creep. Instead of running for the U.S. Senate, perhaps it's time for Mr. Jones to take a little visit to the loony bin."

There is a loud thud as Peter Jones' picture finally drops into the bin.

Another professional voice speaks, "This has been a paid political advertisement by the *Citizens for an Enlightened Government,* a committee to re-elect Jim Ribbons U.S. Senator."

Bernard turns the television off, gets up from the recliner, and walks over to Hoppy, who is now very dirty and sweaty due to his wrangling with the logs. Bernard watches for a few seconds then asks, "What exactly is it that you are doing here?"

Hoppy has just about gotten a large log dragged over to three smaller logs. "I'm getting all my lumber together."

"Why?"

"I'm gonna build a boat."

"You are going to build a boat. Excellent idea. No kidding, really, I mean it. Excellent."

Hoppy smiles. "Thank you."

"And do you intend to make lunch before you build the boat, or after?"

Hoppy smiles again. "You're not trying to be a wise-ass, are you, Bernie?"

"No, no. Just curious."

Hoppy has been wondering about something: "Did you ever wonder why it's so much fun to lay on your back, and look at the sky, and take deep breaths?"

Bernard considers several possible responses, but decides against pursuing this conversation.

* * *

Several hours later, fifteen to twenty logs have been gathered together on the lakeshore. Bernard, back in his recliner, sips another martini and watches television. And Hoppy, nursing a beer, makes lunch.

Bernard is getting hungry. "I wouldn't mind if you finished making that meal sometime today."

"I'm just about done." Hoppy then gets up and goes into his tent, mumbling to himself, "If I can just remember where I left the salt."

Suddenly the words "DCT NEWS SPECIAL REPORT" appear on the screen, followed by a familiar broadcaster seated at his news desk. "Once again, we interrupt our regular programming to bring you the latest news in what officials are now calling the most extensive international manhunt in history.

"The urgency, as we have had it explained to us, is that the contents inside one of the vials stolen from the laboratory of Britain's Institute of Genetic Research could be spilled, or otherwise released, accidentally or on purpose–in which case nothing could prevent the worldwide spread of its mutation within six days. At this time, authorities are saying very little.

"However, DCT News has learned that the identity of the main suspect is known and that he is presently being sought within the borders of the United States."

An unidentified man now walks into the newsroom and hands a sheet of paper to the broadcaster, who then reads from the paper, "Moments ago, at a hastily called news conference, the CIA and the Federal Bureau of Investigation issued a joint statement regarding the identity of the suspect. He is a white male, forty to sixty years old, with blue eyes and brown hair. It is believed he is probably traveling under an alias, and not using his actual birth name: Potato Butt Johnson."

Bernard leaps to his feet and pounds the recliner, hysterical with laughter. "Potato Butt Johnson! Potato Butt Johnson! Oh, geezuz!"

Hoppy, still inside his tent, continues looking for the salt shaker. He appears amused by Bernard's antics. "What's so funny?"

Bernard waves off the question and speaks through his hysterics, "You wouldn't believe it if I told you."

"Okay, well, the soup's ready."

"Soup?"

"Yeah."

Bernard can't believe his ears. "Soup?"

"Yeah."

"You been cooking for an hour and a half, and all you've come up with is soup?"

"That's right, and sometimes it takes two and a half hours–because soup is my specialty."

"What kind of soup is it?"

"Webelo."

Proudly, Hoppy now hands Bernard a bowl of Webelo soup.

Bernard eyes it, then takes a sip. He immediately chokes, coughs, spits, gags, grabs Hoppy's beer and rinses out his mouth, spits, and continues spitting.

He finally recovers enough to evaluate the soup. "That tastes like shit!"

"That's the beauty of it. It's made of highly nutritious animal turds. You can actually survive on this soup."

Bernard looks at Hoppy in astonishment.

"I'm not lying. There was a guy in Montana, Johnny Wilson, 1863, who actually survived for three weeks . . . on squirrel poop."

CHAPTER TEN

Meanwhile, at the Pentagon, ten to fifteen serious men file through high-security subterranean hallways and congregate in a brightly lit conference room. They take their seats behind respective placards reading "CIA," "FBI," "NSA," "KGB," "M15," "INTERPOL," etc. and are presently joined by the five-star general who will preside.

"Good afternoon, gentlemen. I'll get right to the point, as time is of the essence. As you know, yesterday, in a secret laboratory fifty miles outside of London, the one and only vial containing a formula which can alter the behavior of the entire human race . . . was stolen."

The general takes a sip of water and continues, "This formula, which genetically isolates and eliminates all violent tendencies from the human organism, is self-mutating and, assuming it hasn't been contaminated by excessive moisture, would spread itself throughout the entire world within six days of its being released, leaving all of mankind helplessly docile–with the exception of anyone inoculated by the vaccine contained in the one and only other vial, which was stolen at the same time. From here on, the code words to distinguish between the two vials will be either Red Label–for the behavior-changing formula–or Blue Label–for the vaccine."

Before continuing, the general pauses for a full dramatic effect. "I'm certain that I don't have to expound on the disastrous consequences of a worst-case scenario, other than to say we–and by 'we,' I mean the entire world population, the entire human race, we, every single goddamn one of us–would immediately become passive slaves to whoever is still capable of being violent. That is to say, the only person or persons inoculated with the vaccine."

The general wipes his forehead. "Now, at this time, we believe we know the identity of the man who stole the vials. However, we do not yet know his motive: whether he acted alone and it was simply a crime of opportunity–or whether he is part of a criminal conspiracy or a terrorist plot planning to take over and rule the entire planet. The suspect has no previous criminal record or history of trouble other than a shooting incident at at the age of nine.

"At present, we are in the process of running DNA tests on blood found at the scene of the crime and hairs taken from the pillow of the suspect's bed, a suspect whom we were able to tentatively identify through a custom's photo. We should know by 0900 hours if the DNA match is confirmed. If so, then all agencies will be focused on him alone."

He takes off his glasses and rubs his eyes. "Gentlemen, all of mankind is depending on us to either capture or kill this man before it's too late. God be with us."

CHAPTER ELEVEN

At the *Chicago International Airport*, Clayton and Tiffany disembark from their plane. They walk into the terminal and turn down a hallway where a computerized-schedule-board reads: "UNITED Flight 118" NOW BOARDING for ANCHORAGE ALASKA.

* * *

The scientist at the British science-laboratory who made the call to the United States, along with two very sinister-looking men, enter the London airport. They pass under a schedule-board that reads: "BRITISH Flight 224 JUST ARRIVED," and continue directly down the hallway to a boarding counter where the clerk stamps their tickets before they enter the gate that has a schedule-board above it that reads: "ANCHORAGE ALASKA Flight 147 NOW BOARDING."

* * *

Hoppy is on the lakeshore, still hard at work, attempting to pull two of the accumulated logs tightly together. Grunting and straining, he finally succeeds and beams with happiness. He then proceeds with the next step in his efforts to build his boat: the lashing of the timber. Hoppy goes to his backpack and pulls out a one-hundred-foot tightly wrapped clothesline. He searches the nearby area and finds four perfect rocks the approximate size of baseballs. His pace quickens.

He returns to his backpack and pulls out a book: *The Webelo Handbook for Survival.*

And now, at long last, Hoppy is about to enter the final stages of his boat building project.

Hoppy anxiously opens the handbook to a page titled, in big letters, "THE WEBELO RAFT." He props up the book within the grip of a perfect, four-rock arrangement, which allows him to easily view "THE WEBELO RAFT" and the uncomplicated diagram of curving rope-arrows just below it.

He darts to the lake and splashes his face, returns to the logs, and stretches out his muscles. He then jogs in place, taking deep breaths until he is fully invigorated for the task ahead. Squatting close to the logs, the rope, and the handbook, Hoppy reaches into his pocket, pulls out his Swiss Army knife, unfolds its miniature scissors, and, measuring exactly two arms-length, four times, he cuts off a section of clothes-line.

Hoppy studies the diagram: It appears that the rope is supposed to go up and over the first log, back and around the second log, down and between both logs, and back up to where the two ends can then be knotted together. Thus, mentally imprinted with these instructions, Hoppy advances, lash in hand.

Without hesitation, he takes one end of the rope and wraps it down and around both logs. But immediately realizes his mistake, and so tries again.

And again.

Bernard has been watching Hoppy and can't believe what he has just seen. Getting out of the recliner, he turns the television off and approaches Hoppy. "Tell me you're kidding."

Hoppy looks up at him. "What?"

"Tell me you're kidding. Tell me you're not really trying to tie the same knot that's pictured on that page."

"Yeah, I am. That's the special knot we use for the Webelo raft. It's actually called the 'Webelo knot.' I used to be pretty darn good at it. Great, actually." He smiles proudly. "At one time, when I was a kid, I could take a piece of string and tie a Webelo knot before Jeff and Ernie, my cousins from Gardnerville, could jump off the chicken coop and run three times around the tractor."

Bernard is stunned by this news. "Hoppy, listen to me carefully." He pauses before continuing, "Are you listening?"

Hoppy nods that he is listening.

"You, Hoppy Johnson, are what normal people refer to as . . . a moron."

This breaks Hoppy up, and once he stops laughing, he responds with a friendly punch to Bernard's shoulder. "Good one. I owe you."

Bernard shrugs and then ambles over to the lake, gazing off to the distant island two miles away. "So, after you get your little boat built, then what?"

Hoppy indicates to the island in the middle of the lake. "I want to sail it out to that island out there."

"Why?

"Because."

"'Cause why."

"Just 'cause."

Bernard is once again reminded of an old 'curiosity.' "Really, didn't you ever wonder why we hang around together?"

"No."

"I have."

"Why do we?"

Bernard shakes his head. "I'm afraid to actually verbalize it."

"Why?"

"Because once you hear something said 'out loud' it becomes sort of . . . official."

"So?"

"So, I don't think I'm quite ready to hear that you and I hang around together because we are both on the same . . . intellectual level."

Hoppy just smiles. "Why? Even if we're not . . . you're still a smart enough guy."

Bernard shakes his head and returns to his recliner.

And now, this time with enough concentration to make his eyes narrow, Hoppy reviews the diagram. Then, maintaining his steely concentration, he successfully lashes the first two logs, ties the Webelo knot, and pumps the air with his fist. "Yes!"

Bernard watches television as Hoppy is heard in the background, tying more logs together.

On the television screen, two guests are about to be introduced on an afternoon talk show. The host begins. "Today we are going to take a look at a phenomenon which psychologists are now calling the most serious social problem of our time . . . intolerance. The unwillingness to consider another person's point of view. Our guests today include Professor Thurman Oswald, the well-known behavioral-psychologist from Harvard University, who agrees one hundred percent with the Freudian conclusions placing the problem of intolerance on the contradictory signals that a child receives during his early potty training.

"Our other guest is the esteemed author of the best-selling book, *How to Overcome Bigotry, Bias, Prejudice, Dogmatism, and*

Narrow-Mindedness. He's also the recipient of the Fredrick William Johnson Award for his recently published theories on how to promote trust and understanding through the process of confrontational interaction. Welcome, Dr. Clyde Buchanon. Thank you, gentlemen, for being here today."

They nod cordially, and the host continues, "Let's start with you, Professor Oswald. Can you tell us why it is that in this period of humankind's greatest intellectual accomplishments," he says while animating his arms, "space probes to the end of the solar system, laser beams that can cut through steel, computers that transmit fifty trillion bits of data per second, and so on and so forth."

He now begs dramatically for an answer: "Why is it that the human being is still a violent species languishing in a primitive state of racial intolerance, religious intolerance, cultural intolerance, and gender intolerance . . . why?" He now uncoils from his theatrics. "How can human-kind be so brilliant and yet be so stupid at the same time?"

The professor widens his eyes and takes a deep breath. "Well, it seems to me that the root of the problem can be traced back to the earliest years of a child's life when he is first scolded for soiling his diapers. The anti-social message that you are a bad person for committing this very natural act . . . implants the seed of latent hostility. And it is this very seed that later develops into the intolerance so prevalent in today's society."

The host now addresses Dr. Buchanon, who has moved onto the edge of his chair, anticipating his turn to speak. "Dr. Buchanon?"

Dr. Buchanon responds, "Well, to begin with, let me just say that Professor Oswald is completely full of shit."

The professor yanks off his glasses. "Up yours, Buchanon, you left-wing, fetus-murdering, welfare-loving, devil-worshiping bastard."

Buchanon jumps up and throws his chair at Oswald. "Try this on for size, you schizophrenic son-of-a-bitch."

At this point, the show is interrupted by another DCT NEWS SPECIAL REPORT.

The familiar broadcaster appears. "We interrupt this program to bring you the latest news in that frightening story out of London, England. Authorities are now saying they believe the main suspect, a Mr. Potato Butt Johnson, is part of a small terrorist group operating out of Reno, Nevada."

Bernard reacts. "Wow! A homeboy!" He yells back over his shoulder to Hoppy, "Get over here and listen to this!"

Hoppy maintains his concentration on building the raft. "Can't. I'm busy."

The broadcaster continues, "More information is becoming known by the hour. It appears that Mr. Johnson may be in the company of another man, as yet unidentified, but who is assumed to be an armed and extremely dangerous accomplice. Although the authorities are said to prefer capturing the suspects alive, federal agents have been issued 'shoot to kill' orders should it be necessary to prevent the release of the unstoppable, self-mutating substance, which is believed to still be in their possession.

"That is the latest information known at this time. Stay tuned to this station as we will be bringing you updates on this story as the news breaks. This is Ralph Jensen for DCT News Special Report."

Bernard clicks the television off, stands, stretches, approaches Hoppy, and indicates back to the television. "You're really missing something great."

Hoppy has been busy, and now, with five logs lashed together, the project is actually starting to look like a seaworthy raft. "What did you say?"

Bernard, "Oh nothing. Just the greatest news story ever."

"What happened?"

"Oh, nothing much–except that the entire world is involved in a manhunt for a couple of idiots who have in their possession the means to turn every human being on the planet into a gerbil."

"What are you talking about?"

"It's a long story. Forget about it."

"What happened?"

"Forget about it. Build your boat. You can watch the six o'clock news. They'll have the whole story."

"But, what happened? It sounds important."

"Forget it. It's nothing. The cops are gonna shoot a couple of idiots, and everything'll be fine." Bernard pulls out a cigar. "Build your boat." He lights the cigar.

CHAPTER TWELVE

The scientist and his two sinister companions make their way across a terminal, up an escalator, and into another terminal, where a computerized high-tech-verbalization voice is heard. "Flight 721 to Anchorage, Alaska is now boarding at gate 15."

On a remote airstrip, Clayton and Tiffany toss their handbags into a waiting helicopter with the words GRIZZLY BEAR AIRLINES lettered across its fuselage.

The helicopter is soon skimming over the wilderness when the pilot speaks back over his shoulder, "Can I ask you something?"

Clayton answers for both of them. "Sure, go ahead and ask."

"What the heck would ever possess a person to go to Last Chance, Alaska?"

Clayton smiles, "With us, it's a religious calling. We go wherever people need to hear the word of God."

The pilot looks into the rear-view mirror, "I figured it must be something like that."

Clayton smiles saintly up into the mirror.

Before long, the pilot is once again compelled to speak. "I hope you don't mind, but I'd like to give you a little advice just for your own good."

Clayton responds, "Go ahead, I'd be grateful to hear it."

"Well, I was just gonna say that I don't think you want to be doin' too much of that religious stuff around Shorty."

"Who's Shorty?"

"Shorty's an atheist. An interesting guy but probably a little high-strung for most people's taste. He runs the Last Chance Hotel. His wife used to run the restaurant, but she died a few years back. Christmas Eve. Flew into Anchorage for the 'midnight mass.' Got one of those little communion-wafers caught in her throat. Choked to death. Shorty hasn't been the same ever since."

* * *

On the lakeshore, Hoppy finishes lashing the final log, and the raft is now a completed project: a ten-foot square platform of tightly bound logs. He stands back to admire his work and sip a cup of coffee. "It's finally finished. I've been waiting twenty-five years to build a Webelo raft, and now I've done it."

Bernard is in the recliner, swiveled to watch Hoppy work on his raft. He sips a martini. The television has been turned off. He questions the value of the raft. "You've been waiting twenty-five years to build that thing?"

"Yep. I just wish my Uncle Mort were here to see it. He'd have been proud."

"Where is your Uncle Mort?"

"Dead. Died a long time ago. Tetanus."

"Step on a rusty nail?"

"Harpoon."

Bernard is brought to a halt by this information, which he believes to be too weird and requires further explanation. "Your Uncle Mort stepped on a rusty harpoon?"

Hoppy is visibly upset by the question but manages an explanation after pointing to his own butt. "It was a shooting incident. It's a long story. A sad story. It was all my fault. It's the worst thing that ever happened in my entire life. I was only nine years old at the time. But still, to this day, it's too painful to even talk about." He hangs his head. "Every time I even think of it . . . it rips my guts out."

Bernard can see the sadness in Hoppy's face, and, respecting his pain, he drops the subject by swiveling his chair squarely around to the lake. He's soon lost in thought.

Hoppy, still in the throes of having his guts ripped out by the mere recollection of Mort's demise, goes to his backpack and extracts a brush and a small can of red paint.

He then returns to the raft and kneels next to it, opens the can of paint, and looks to the heavens. "This one's for you, Uncle Mort."

Having spoken, Hoppy now makes his tribute visible by painting "THE MORT" on the side of the raft. Taking a deep emotional breath after finishing, Hoppy puts the can of paint and the brush aside and proceeds to build a campfire. First, some wood must be gathered, and this is accomplished within a matter of seconds. Then comes the hard part: starting the fire by striking two flint-stones together (which assumably is, probably, a Webelo-thing).

As Hoppy unsuccessfully strikes away, Bernard's recliner swivels slowly back around until Bernard faces Hoppy's backside. After a very genuine effort to refrain from re-introducing the hurtful subject, Bernard is overcome by curiosity: "I know it's a very painful thing to talk about . . . but I would really, really appreciate it if you could bring yourself to tell me how your Uncle Mort got tetanus from a harpoon."

Hoppy is too distraught to respond.

However, Bernard absolutely must hear the rest of this sad tale. "May I just take a guess? And then you can just tell me if I'm right or wrong. You can just nod yes or no. You won't even have to speak. Okay? Here's my guess. Did you accidentally shoot your Uncle Mort in the ass with a harpoon when you were a Webelo?"

There is a pause before Hoppy shakes his head. "No."

"What part did I get wrong? It did happen when you were a Webelo, right?"

Hoppy nods. "Yes."

"You did do the shooting?"

Hoppy nods. "Yes."

"You did hit him in the ass?"

Hoppy nods. "Yes."

"What part did I get wrong? You accidentally shot your Uncle Mort in the ass with a harpoon when you were a Webelo–" He pauses, reviewing what he just said. "Oh my God! You shot him . . . on purpose?"

Hoppy nods shamefully. "Yes."

Bernard is aghast. "That's murder! You murdered your Uncle Mort!"

Hoppy meekly defends himself, "I didn't think he would die. I was just trying to teach him a lesson."

"A lesson! What kind of lesson?! How to catch a harpoon with your ass?!"

Hoppy finally feels the need for further explanation. "I just wanted him to know that he should mind his own business when parents are deciding on what to name their baby. And that no matter what . . . he should never again even attempt to convince somebody that their kid would someday appreciate the originality of being named . . . Potato Butt."

Bernard is stunned into silence as Hoppy returns to striking his flint stones.

Inevitably, there comes time for the follow-up question. And Bernard asks it, "Did you just 'get me'?"

Hoppy doesn't understand the question. "Huh?"

Bernard repeats himself, "Did you just 'get me'?"

Hoppy still has no clue of what Bernard is talking about. "Huh?"

Bernard appears to be in a panic. "Remember when I said you were a moron and you said that you owed me one . . . did you just pay me back?"

"I have no idea what you're talking about."

Bernard swivels around and, voicing his fear, clicks the television on to search for a news report. "Omigod. Omigod. Oooomigod."

On CNN, Ernest Cooper is wrapping up the broadcast, "That's it for now. Stay tuned to this station for continuing coverage of the terrorist manhunt."

Bernard yells at Hoppy, "Ohhhhh!"

Hoppy is pre-occupied with the small wisp of smoke now rising from the campfire.

Bernard frantically hunts for another news station.

A FOX newscaster appears on the screen. "The whole world has been talking about it for the last two days. Now, FOX News brings you an exclusive interview with the man who made the positive identification on the second suspect . . . the one that authorities now believe may be the mastermind of terrorist activities throughout the world. FOX will also bring you an exclusive interview with the stool pigeon whose information has lead authorities to narrow their search to a particular area of the Alaskan wilderness. To begin tonight's story, let's go to Jim Stevens at the El Dorado Hotel-Casino in Reno, Nevada . . . from where this terrorist is said to have plotted his activities."

Standing outside the El Dorado Hotel-Casino, microphone in hand, Jim Stevens reports: "Thank you, Mark. Standing just to the right of me, here in the heart of this vibrant city of neon lights and gambling tables, is Neil Bartly, the man who identified the so-called 'Mastermind of Evil.'" Turning to Neil (AKA the Big Dog), Jim continues, "Mr. Bartly, could you tell us what you know about this mysterious terrorist?"

Neil enjoys the moment, "Yeah, I'll be happy to tell you. He's a beady-eyed little weasel named Bernard L. Latrell, and he ought to be shot on sight."

"Thank you, Mr. Bartly. And here on my left is Raymond Rochette, the bartender who informed authorities as to the suspects' exact location, and who, within the past week, actually served drinks to both of the suspected terrorists." Jim turns to Raymond. "Mr. Rochette, could you give us your impressions of this Latrell character?"

"He was kind of a quiet man, well mannered, yet the sort of gentleman who spent a great deal of time in brothels carousing with prostitutes. And of course, I was quite shocked to learn that Mr. Latrell is also the man responsible for causing so much pain and suffering."

Jim nods. "And I understand you have a book coming out that reveals many shocking details of Mr. Latrell's wicked and scandalous life."

Raymond is eager to hype his book. "That is correct, Jim. The book is titled *The Webelo Drank Martinis*, and it will be in your local bookstores no later than two o'clock tomorrow afternoon."

Jim 'throws it back' to the anchorman: "This is Jim Stevens, reporting from the terrorist's own playground."

Bernard is now in a state of shock. His mouth hangs open, and he appears to have a death grip on the armrests of his recliner.

Hoppy notices. "What's the matter? Bad news?"

CHAPTER THIRTEEN

The scientist and his two sinister companions approach a helicopter warming its motor just outside a hangar. They each toss a duffle bag into the cargo bay then climb aboard. The helicopter lifts off.

Seated next to their duffle bags, beyond the scope of the pilot's view, the two companions begin to reveal the contents of the bags. The first companion unpacks and assembles an expensive-looking long-barrelled handgun. The second companion unpacks and assembles an AK-47. Then, with the 'weapons check' complete, they each reverse the process and put the weapons back into their duffle bags.

Curiously, the scientist runs his thumb slowly across the face of his wristwatch.

* * *

In a forest clearing, Clayton and Tiffany stand with their bags on frozen mud, looking at an old, weather-beaten, two-story wooden structure with a piece of cardboard reading "Last Chance Hotel" nailed to its front door.

After studying the hotel at length, Clayton indicates to Tiffany that it is safe to advance.

They approach and enter.

The lobby is empty.

Clayton sets the bags down, crosses to the registration desk, and rings the little bell next to the old black and white TV with the rabbit-ears antenna. The sound is off, but the picture is on. Shortly, from upstairs, footsteps are heard.

Then a man, Shorty, with a six-shooter strapped to his hip, a hunting knife in the unbuckled sheath strapped to his other hip, and a hammer in his hand, descends the stairs, smoking a cigarette. He stands four feet, zero inches.

He approaches Clayton, who sticks out a friendly hand. Shorty ignores the gesture, walks up close to Clayton's stomach, and–without looking up–motions with a finger for Clayton to lower his face to Shorty's level. Clayton good-naturedly responds by squatting on his haunches.

Eyeball to eyeball, Shorty speaks, "You a religious man?"

Clayton considers his words before speaking, "Sorry to disappoint you, but I happen to be an atheist."

Shorty gives him another look, then approaches Tiffany.

Standing close to her breasts, he then motions her to his level, and she bends down.

Shorty gives her the 'once over.' "You a religious woman?"

Tiffany considers her words. Then looks Shorty in the eyes. "I believe in love. Period."

Shorty turns away, walks over to the registration desk, and directs himself to Clayton. "Five bucks a night. Cash. In advance."

Clayton pulls a five-dollar bill out of his wallet and hands it to Shorty. "One night."

Shorty points up the stairs. "Second floor, first door on your right."

Clayton motions to Tiffany, and they head upstairs.

* * *

Bernard and Hoppy race along the shoreline before flopping against a tree to catch their breath.

Hoppy apologizes, "Sorry about that back there."

Bernard is panting like a dog. "You're sorry? You're sorry? We had one stinkin' chance, one possible chance to get out of this alive–and you screwed it up!"

Hoppy feels terrible about 'screwing up.' "Geez, I didn't do it on purpose. I said I was sorry. What else can I say?"

"Nothin'. Nothin'. Just fuckin' nothin'."

"Okay, so let's just put it behind us and concentrate on what we should do now. I still think we've got to get out to that island and call the police and tell them there's been a mistake. You agree?"

"Hoppy, let me explain the basic difference between an island . . . and places where one can go when not in possession of a boat." Bernard exaggerates a smile for effect. "It is Hoppy isn't it? Your other name?"

"Actually, it's my nickname. Potato Butt *is* my legal name."

"Great. Now, what was I saying?"

"You were going to tell me about the difference between–"

"Shaddup!"

Snarling with sarcasm, Bernard jogs off with Hoppy following close behind. "And just a little advice for the future. Before building your next ten-ton boat on the shore of a lake . . . give some thought as to how you might actually get it over to the fuckin' water."

* * *

The scientist and his two companions, each holding a duffle bag, stand on the frozen ground in front of the hotel, under a canopy of stars twinkling in the coal-black sky. After a lengthy scrutiny, the scientist leads one of them off towards the door and motions the other off into the shadows.

CHAPTER THIRTEEN

* * *

Clayton is in the shower, all soaped up. Tiffany sits on the bed in the dimly-lit adjacent room. The bathroom door is open, and Clayton converses with her. "There's nothing like a hot shower after a long plane ride. You sure you don't want to join me?"

"No. I happen to be very nervous at the moment."

"Nothing to be nervous about. I'm gonna give them whatever it is I picked up in England, and they're gonna give me a million dollars, and that's about all there is to it."

At this point, Tiffany shields her movements from Clayton's line of sight and takes two vials out of her bra. She then peels the red label off the first vial and presses it onto the other vial, then she peels off the blue label and presses it onto the first vial.

(Unspoken speculation about the consequences of switching labels enhances the drama of this circumstance.)

* * *

Accompanied by one of his companions, the scientist enters the front door and crosses the lobby to the registration desk. His companion moves off to the corner of the room, removes his topcoat, and lays it over his folded arms. The scientist rings the desk-bell.

Smoking a cigarette, Shorty descends the stairs. He looks at the scientist, then at his companion. Then, after some inner deliberation, he approaches the companion. Facing off from a distance of five feet, Shorty and the companion feel each other out with their eyes.

Finally, the companion speaks without emotion. "Fuck you, shorty."

Shorty backs off, turns away, and walks around toward the registration desk.

Then–once he has the scientist positioned between himself and the companion–Shorty casually draws his gun and, using the scientist as his shield, fires once, hitting the companion right between the eyes. The hidden AK-47 falls from his folded arms as the companion drops to the floor.

The scientist turns to Shorty and speaks without concern for his dead companion, "My associate should have arrived within the past few hours . . . could you please tell him that Thomas Brown is waiting for him in the lobby."

Shorty considers the request, then heads upstairs with the message.

In room two, Tiffany answers the knock at the door, and Shorty delivers the message, "Thomas Brown's in the lobby."

Tiffany closes the door and walks into the steamy bathroom, where Clayton stands half-dressed in front of a mirror, combing his hair. Tiffany relays the message, "Thomas Brown is waiting in the lobby."

Clayton is not rushed by this news and continues to comb his hair.

* * *

Three CIA men stand near Hoppy's raft, surmising the meaning of the evidence: a raft, a recliner, a television set, a suitcase full of liquor, tent equipment, and a campfire.

The first CIA man makes the obvious assessment. "They can't have gotten too far. Their campfire is still warm."

The CIA officer in charge gives an order, "Call the general. We'll follow their footprints."

With this much said and done, they chase off.

Meanwhile, Hoppy and Bernard, running hard and breathing hard, decide to 'take five.' Bernard splashes lake-water onto his face. Hoppy crawls up onto a large boulder overhanging the lake to have a look around. A full moon lights their surroundings.

Bernard shrieks. "Oh my God!"

Hoppy snaps into high-alert. "What's the matter?"

Bernard points to an old wooden rowboat, with oars aboard, bobbing in the water. "It's a miracle!"

Hoppy looks down at the water below him and sees the rowboat.

Bernard is bursting with excitement. "It's a miracle! We can get to the island! We can get to a telephone! We can straighten out this whole mess! We're gonna live! We're gonna live!"

Hoppy is ecstatic. "Yahoo!"

Bernard quickly instructs Hoppy before wading out to untie the rope that's mooring the rowboat. "Get down here! Hurry up!"

Hoppy, beside himself with joy, jumps from the boulder down into the rowboat, and, once his feet have broken through the hull, is left standing in the water with the rowboat up around his waist.

Bernard explodes into a fist-pumping rage. "That does it! I'm gonna kick your ass! Get over here! Right now! Get over here!"

At this point, Bernard notices that Hoppy's attention is focused on some circumstance seemingly unrelated to the boating incident.

Bernard turns to see what could possibly be of more concern than the immediate threat of having one's ass kicked . . . and finds himself the object of three rigidly aimed weapons. "Oh my God."

One of the CIA men shouts, "Freeze! You too, Potato Butt!"

Bernard and Hoppy throw up their hands. Bernard speaks for both of them, "Okay, okay! Stay calm! Don't shoot!"

"Where's the goods Latrell?" another CIA man shouts.

Bernard attempts to politely disagree. "We don't have any goods, sir. There's been a mistake. We're not the crooks, sir."

The CIA man responds with an exaggerated smile, "Really?"

Bernard smiles back. "Really. Swear to God."

The CIA man introduces a trace of sarcasm into the conversation. "Okay, Latrell. But before we let you go . . . would you mind explaining to us how the DNA from the blood at the crime scene matches the DNA of Potato Butt's pillow hairs, taken from Potato Butt's trailer."

Bernard thinks for a moment or two, looks at Hoppy, longs for an answer, but Hoppy can only shrug. "I dunno."

Another CIA man talks into his cell phone. "They're stonewalling. We'll bring 'em in."

He then passes along the instructions from the top of the CIA's chain-of-command. "The general says if they make one false move on the way in . . . shoot the bastards."

Bernard gulps. "What would be the best way for me to move without having it 'misconstrued' as . . . false?"

As the suspects are getting cuffed, one of the CIA men advises, "If it were me, I'd try to keep a smile on my face. A big one."

CHAPTER FOURTEEN

Back at the Last Chance Hotel, Clayton, now fully dressed, makes one last trip to the bathroom to pat his cheeks with cologne.

Tiffany approaches him. Her eyes are steady and demand the truth. "And this money, this million-dollars, it's all going to be given to an organization that helps sick and homeless children . . . correct?"

Clayton looks at Tiffany's reflection in the mirror. "Are you doubting me?"

Tiffany, maybe for the first time, understands his evasiveness for what it is. "I've doubted you for a long time Clayton."

Clayton smiles, turns, and walks out of the bathroom, giving Tiffany's butt a little pat as he passes by.

He crosses the room, opens the door, and gestures to Tiffany that it is time for them to go.

The hotel lobby is sparse but not empty of drama:

There's a scientist waiting for some kind of contraband.

A dead body is in the corner of the lobby.

And there's a feisty short man behind the desk.

Now, with Tiffany on his arm, Clayton descends the stairway.

Leaving Tiffany off at the bottom, Clayton approaches the scientist, who offers a handshake. Clayton declines the handshake with a nod of his head, and the scientist withdraws his hand.

The two are face-to-face, and the scientist speaks first, "How do you want to do this, Clay?"

Clayton eyes the dead body in the corner. "Set the bag of money on the floor. Opened."

The scientist does as directed. Clayton takes a glance at the money, then indicates for Tiffany to bring him the two vials. Tiffany does. Clayton then sets the two vials on the floor near the money.

The scientist starts to bend down to pick up the vials, but Clayton stops him with a firm touch on the shoulder. "Not yet."

The scientist rises back up. "What's on your mind, Clay?"

Clay tells him. "I wanna know what's in those vials."

The scientist considers his answer. "You've probably been a little too busy these last couple of days to read the newspapers or watch TV, right?"

Clay nods. "I'd say so."

The scientist informs him: "Well, if you'd had any access to the news, you'd know that a formula for a new and improved aspirin has been discovered . . . and stolen. And it's worth . . . who knows . . . one million? Two million? Ten million? Maybe nothing.

"Who knows how much a pharmaceutical company would pay to get it back? Maybe the whole deal would go bad and somebody would get killed or end up going to prison for twenty years. It's the chance you take. Sometimes you make it. Sometimes you don't. My father used to say, 'The smart ones always take the sure thing, and use it to enjoy their life.' I'd say a million dollars cash without the risk of death or jail would be a sure thing. Wouldn't you agree?"

Clayton considers a few things and then indicates for the scientist to go ahead and pick up the vials.

The scientist acts accordingly, and, as he stoops to pick up the vials, he also takes a hypodermic needle out from under his coat.

With his foot, Clayton then nudges the duffle-bag full of money over next to the desk and instructs Shorty, "Take as much as you can get in one handful."

Shorty remains seated behind the desk. "I don't need no money."

Clayton retrieves the duffle bag. "Suit yourself. Not all atheists think alike."

Case in hand, Clayton offers his arm to Tiffany, and she joins him. But just before they reach the door, it bursts open, and the scientist's companion with the long-barrelled handgun is suddenly facing them. Stepping inside, the man motions with the gun for Clayton and Tiffany to back up.

They do.

The scientist motions toward Shorty. "Watch out for the shrimp, he's armed."

The companion aims his gun at Shorty. "Stand up."

Shorty stands. The companion commands again. "Now, with your left hand, take your gun out of the holster, and slowly set it on the floor."

Shorty obeys.

"Now, take your foot and slide that pre-historic piece of shit over here."

Shorty obeys.

"So, you're the one who did him?" he says, nodding to the dead body in the corner of the lobby.

Shorty replies, "That's right."

"You saved me a bullet." Now, the companion turns to Clayton. "You shouldn't have called me a donkey. It's not polite."

Striking fast and hard, the companion back-hands Clayton across the face. Clayton's nose breaks, and blood pours out. "Now, before I get down to the fun of stomping my boot heel through your face," he says, before turning the gun at the scientist, "Now I've got a little business to do with Tom. What's in those vials Tom, that makes them worth you paying one hundred thousand dollars for two bodyguards for two days?"

Tom, the scientist, smiles. "I'll be happy to tell you." He takes out a cigarette. "If you hadn't been so busy with me during these last two days, you would have heard the news reports about the formula for a new, greatly improved aspirin, that has been discovered." He lights the cigarette. "And stolen." He takes a long drag. "And, just now, handed over in exchange for the one million dollars that is in that duffle bag." He motions to the bag in Clayton's hand.

The companion now turns his gun and his attention back to Clayton.

The scientist continues, "And so, the fact that you have a gun aimed at the man who possesses the million dollars means that if you wanted that money for yourself . . . you could probably have it." He takes another long drag. "As a matter of fact, you could take that bag full of money, use up three bullets, and be out of here before," he says as he pulls back his shirt sleeve back to have a look at his wristwatch, "before nine o'clock."

To emphasize the time frame of his plan, the scientist holds his bent wrist up to his companion, and with his fore-finger, casually taps his wristwatch. Instantly, the wristwatch recoils as it fires a tiny bullet into the companion's forehead, dropping him in his tracks.

The scientist indicates to the duffle bag, then rolls up his sleeve and ties a rubber tourniquet on his arm in preparation for a hypodermic injection. "Go ahead, Clay. It's yours. Take it. Enjoy your life."

Clayton nods his thanks and pulls a handkerchief from his pocket to clean the blood off his face.

The scientist inserts the hypodermic needle into the blue vial and sucks out all the fluid. He then inserts the needle into his arm and empties the syringe.

Shorty notices. "Hey, what're you doin'?"

The scientist speaks, "I got a headache."

Shorty immediately understands. "Hey, wait a minute. I know what you're doing. I watch TV, and those," he says, pointing at the vials, "those are the vials that everybody's looking for." He squints. "And you're Potato Butt Johnson ain't ya?!"

Shorty now has Clayton and Tiffany's full attention. "Some scientists in England discovered a way to make everybody in the world non-violent. And at the same time, they developed a vaccine for it. And that's what's in the vials." He turns to the scientist. "The vaccine that will allow you to be the only violent person left in the world . . . that's what you just injected into your arm, ain't it?"

The scientist unties the tourniquet and rolls his sleeve back down. "That's right." He now takes the remaining vial and drops it onto the floor where it shatters into pieces, releasing a small pool of liquid.

Then, indicating to the liquid, the scientist explains the situation to Clayton: "Within six days that unstoppable, self-mutating, small puddle of liquid, will render every human being on this planet passive and unable to defend themselves from the one person still willing and able to be violent . . . me, the vaccinated person. Me, the one and only person that everyone must obey. Me. Just, me. And there is nothing anyone can do about it now. So, go ahead, take your million dollars, and enjoy it while you can . . . because after six days from now, you're gonna be just like everybody else. Just one of my servants."

Clayton is stunned by the turn of events. He considers the situation and starts to speak, but is interrupted by the scientist. "Forget it, Clay. There is no more vaccine."

Clayton and the scientist lock eyes, and a decision is made. Clayton lets the bag drop onto the floor, gives Tiffany a brief cold stare, then walks out the door.

Tiffany turns to the scientist. "May I have the money?"

The scientist approaches Tiffany, and with a little smile, reaches out and gives one of her breasts a squeeze. "Go ahead."

Tiffany picks up the duffle bag, and as she opens the door to leave, she pauses briefly to hear the scientist's parting remark. "Maybe I'll give you a call sometime . . . some rainy Tuesday afternoon when I'm bored with thirteen-year-old virgins."

Tiffany gives him an odd sort of smile, then leaves.

The scientist now turns to Shorty. "You're kind of a smart little fella. I might just leave you completely alone, right here where you are." He buttons his sleeve. "It all depends on how comfortable you can make me while I'm your guest for the next six days."

* * *

On television sets all around the world, regular programming is interrupted by a late-breaking special report. Shorty turns the volume up as Ralph Pelley's broadcast begins; "Good evening. Details are still sketchy at this time. However, it has now been confirmed that Potato Butt Johnson was captured along with his accomplice, a shadowy figure known among international terrorists as . . . 'the Webelo.'"

The screen then shows a convoy of security vehicles whizzing past a crowd of reporters and entering a heavily guarded military compound, with Hoppy and Bernard visible in the back seat of one of the vehicles.

Potato Butt waves his cuffed hands. Bernard's face is one big frozen smile. Pelley continues his report, "Approximately one hour ago, in a daring raid on the terrorists' Alaskan hideaway, a CIA special ops unit–"

* * *

The TV in the lobby of the Last Chance Hotel abruptly stops working as the scientist yanks on its cord. "I'll be up in my room. I'd like some dinner. Now." He then heads up the stairs.

CHAPTER FIFTEEN

The following summer, dressed in their black pants, white shirts, bow ties, gold-embroidered vests, and aprons, Bernard and Hoppy ride up the El Dorado Hotel-Casino escalator. Bernard reads the "Sporting News."

Hoppy has an idea. "You know what I think?"

Bernard responds without taking his nose out of the newspaper. "Dying to know."

Hoppy has made a decision. "I'm going to ask that girl to marry me."

Bernard is moderately curious. "The one with the big tits?"

"No. The one that gave a million bucks to that orphanage. Lulabell," Hoppy says in regard to Tiffany, who has finally started using her real name.

Bernard mumbles, "Good idea."

"Don't you think she and I are totally made for each other?"

"Yes. You are definitely," he looks up from the newspaper, "birds of a feather."

Hoppy smiles. "Did you notice the way she was looking at me when I was telling her about my dreams for the future?"

Bernard pulls the newspaper higher up around his head. "When you said that you wanted to build a chicken farm for homeless children? Yeah, I noticed."

"Can you imagine her finding those vials on the London bridge and then accidentally dropping them into the river? I wonder what would have happened if she hadn't come forward with that information? We'd probably still be in prison."

At this point, the Big Dog is about to pass Bernard on the descending side of the escalator. "You chewing gum, Latrell?"

Bernard has his head buried so deeply into the newspaper as to be completely out of view. "No."

Bernard steps off the escalator and, with Hoppy trailing close behind, heads for the large busy room with the words EMPLOYEE CAFETERIA lettered on a sign above its doorway. He lowers the newspaper while turning a page, revealing a large bubble of gum protruding from his lips.

Hoppy takes this opportunity to run an idea past Bernard. "I think Lulabell's got a sister. Maybe sometime, the four of us ought to get together. Go camping or something."

Bernard shoots Hoppy an "I don't think so" look.

94

CHAPTER SIXTEEN

A small pontoon-airplane with GRIZZLY BEAR AIRLINES written across its fuselage descends from the sky and lands on a small isolated lake, just a short boat ride away from Last Chance Island.

The plane taxis up to the shoreline to allow its passengers to disembark, and there to meet them are none other than Hoppy Johnson and Bernard L. Latrell. Tents have already been set up, A late afternoon-campfire burns, and a rubber raft is close by, ready to be dragged over to the lake. The bay door opens, and Lulabell and her sister step out. Hoppy greets them. "Hi. It's great to see you again."

Lulabell smiles. "Thank you. It was nice of you to invite us."

Hoppy then indicates to Lulabell's sister, "And this must be your sister, Rocky."

A tough-looking girl in her forty's steps forward. "Yo."

Hoppy now nods at Bernard while Bernard is still reacting to 'yo.' "And this is my best friend, Bernard L. Latrell."

Bernard steps hesitantly forward. "Good evening, ladies."

Lulabell responds, "Good evening."

And Rocky adds her greeting, "Yo."

Hoppy suggests, "Why don't you girls have a seat over there at the campfire, and Bernard and I will unload your gear."

Lulabell smiles, and the girls head off to the campfire.

At this point, the pilot's window slides back, revealing the same pilot who had refused to unload Bernard's bags on his previous trip to Alaska. He speaks matter-of-factly to his former passengers. "The sooner you get things unloaded, the sooner I can get out of here."

Bernard recognizes him and approaches the pilot's window. "Remember me?"

The pilot nods. "Yeah, you're the little shit who left all the litter on your last visit."

Bernard still holds a grudge. "Are you talking about my six-hundred-dollar tent, my nine-hundred-dollar recliner, and my two-thousand-dollar, battery-powered, glare-resistant, television set?"

The pilot looks at him. "Yeah, along with a lot of other crap."

"Where's my TV? I want it back."

The pilot smiles. "Why don't you ask around? Maybe somebody knows something."

Disgusted, Bernard rejoins Hoppy, who is already unloading the plane, and, directing his voice back to the pilot, has the last word, "Once again, thank you for the fine service. I'd tip you, but all I've got on me are nickels, dimes, quarters, halves, dollars, fives, tens, twenties, fifties, and hundreds."

Hoppy hands a large duffle bag to Bernard, and Bernard sets it on the shore.

Then, returning for the next bag, Bernard speaks confidentially to Hoppy, "So what's with the Rocky shit?"

Hoppy takes a moment to think. "Maybe she's the quiet type."

Bernard grumbles. "Or maybe she's the kind who likes her own kind more than our kind."

Hoppy smiles mischievously and hands Bernard another bag. "I hear they make darn good parents."

"I'm hopin' that what I'm thinkin' . . . ain't what is."

Hoppy inquires, "And that would be?"

"That you invited a 'lesbo' out here to be my camping date."

Hoppy cautions against putting too much emphasis on first impressions. "Naw, I don't think so. I think she's just kind of a shy girl. Tomorrow, when we row out to the island for lunch, you'll have a chance to get to know her better. Did I mention that she is the Mayor of Rockyville?"

* * *

The following afternoon, Bernard, Hoppy, Lulabell, and Rocky are in the rubber raft en route to Last Chance Island. Hoppy and Rocky are manning the oars.

Hoppy speaks to Lulabell, "Supposedly, out there on Last Chance Island, there's a three-room hotel with one full-time resident. That should be interesting, doncha think?"

Lulabell smiles. "Could be."

At this point, Bernard casually hangs his arm off the side of the raft to drag his hand through the cool water. And in so doing, inadvertently brushes against Rocky's leg, causing a brief adjustment to her stroke. She reacts by flicking her finger against the back of his head and warning him. "Watch your paws, short stuff."

Bernard gives Hoppy a look that says: "I'll kill you later."

After an hour or so, the foursome arrives at Last Chance Island and pulls their raft ashore. Hoppy is jazzed. "Well, here we are, Last Chance Island. Everybody starving?"

Lulabell answers, "I sure am."

Bernard comments, "I ain't that hungry."

Rocky specifies the extent of her hunger, "I could eat a dead lizard."

In a single facial expression, Bernard offers Hoppy his personal opinion of the moment: "Isn't she lovely."

* * *

98

Bernard then asks, "What time is it getting to be?"

Hoppy glances at his wristwatch. "I dunno, I forgot to wind my watch. It feels kinda early, but it's probably a lot later than we think."

* * *

Somewhere in a middle-eastern desert, fifteen to twenty terrorists and their leader stand near a campfire in a large cave, anticipating the magnitude of what they are about to witness.

Before long, several more men enter the cave. Brief greetings are exchanged and, with huge smiles on their face, the men open an elaborately constructed suitcase and hand its contents to the leader, as they proudly describe their gift.

"We place in your hand one biological weapon of mass destruction capable of killing every living creature on the entire planet. God be praised."

CHAPTER SEVENTEEN

Last Chance Island is in full bloom.

Seated, with his feet propped up on a railing covered with many potted flowers, Shorty relaxes on the hotel's front porch, reading, smoking a cigarette, and having a beer.

He takes the last gulp from his can of beer, pulls a small bell from his vest pocket, and jangles it.

Tom, (the British scientist) comes from inside the hotel to ask, "Are you ready for lunch?"

"What are we having?"

Tom reads from a shortlist, "B.L.T., hold the mayo, and a scoop of vanilla ice cream."

Shorty whines, "We have that every day."

Tom is sympathetic, "It's what you ask for every day."

"Yeah, I know, but I'm tired of it. I want something different."

"Okay. What would you like?"

"How about butter-pecan-sherbet. Do we have that?"

"Sorry. We don't."

"Okay. Fuck it. Just gimme the vanilla."

Tom nods, "Okay, one B. L. T., hold the mayo, and a scoop of vanilla ice cream coming right up." He pauses to inhale the fragrance of a potted flower. "And by the way, don't forget it's the Fourth of July, the day you promised to quit smoking."

Shorty grunts. "I'll do it tomorrow."

Tom admonishes, "Shorty..."

Shorty whines again, "Okay. Geezuz. Quit naggin'."

"I'm not nagging. I just want what's best for you. And Shorty, I eventually intend to be your friend, whether you like it or not."

Tom leaves to make lunch.

* * *

Hoppy, Lulabell, Rocky, and Bernard walk out of the forest into this meadow of bright flowers spread out around the hotel.

Hoppy and Lulabell hold hands. Bernard and Rocky, separated by ten feet of defensible space, appear to be somewhere between bored and irritated.

Looking through the hotel's kitchen window, Tom notices this small group and immediately walks outside to welcome them. Wiping his hands on his apron, he speaks to Shorty as he descends the porch stairs to head off across the meadow. "We have guests."

Shorty looks up from his book, clearly annoyed by this interruption to his day.

As Tom nears the guests, he suddenly recognizes Lulabell and breaks into a huge smile, and quickens his step with his arms wide open.

Reaching her, he wraps her in a loving bear hug. Lulabell hugs him back as best she can while still holding Hoppy's hand.

Tom speaks, "I'm so sorry for the way I acted the last time I saw you. Forgive me. I am a different person than I was back then."

Lulabell smiles. "I expected you might be. But I'm sorry I don't recall your name."

"Well, when I was a young boy in England, my best chums always called me 'Test Tube Tommy.'"

"That's a mouthful. Mind if I give you a nickname?"

"I would be honored."

Lulabell thinks about it. "How about . . . Beauregard?"

Tom is pleased. "I love it."

Lulabell then moves forward with introductions. "Beauregard, this is my friend Hoppy Johnson. And Hoppy, this is Beauregard."

They shake hands and exchange greetings.

Lulabell turns back to Beauregard, "And this is Hoppy's best friend, Bernard Latrell."

Bernard gives a little salute. Beauregard offers his hand to Bernard. "Nice to meet you, Mr. Latrell."

Lulabell then makes the final introduction. "And, this is my sister, the Mayor of Rockyville, Miss Rocky."

Rocky gives Beauregard a thumbs up. "Yo."

And Beauregard responds, "Very nice to meet you, Rocky."

Beauregard continues, "And now let's all go back to the hotel, and I'll make lunch . . . and your friends can meet Shorty."

Bernard gives Beauregard a glance at the word "Shorty."

Then, once everyone is gathered together on the porch, Beauregard is happy to proceed with introductions. "Shorty, you remember this charming lady, I'm sure."

Shorty gives Lulabell/Tiffany a suspicious look as she smiles back at him.

"And Lulabell," Beauregard continues, "you may not have been formally introduced, but this fine man is Shorty McDonald."

Lulabell reaches out to shake his hand. "Truly, it is very nice to see you again, Mr. McDonald."

Shorty shakes her hand and grunts as Hoppy steps forward. Beauregard still has several more introductions to make. "And this gentleman is Mr. Hoppy Johnson."

Hoppy reaches out to shake hands. Shorty recognizes him, "Potato Butt Johnson?"

Hoppy smiles. "I prefer Hoppy."

Beauregard continues, "And this lovely lady, the Mayor of Rockyville, is Lulabell's sister, Miss Rocky."

Rocky does her thing: "Yo."

"And last but not least, this gentleman is Hoppy's best friend, Mr. Bernard Latrell."

Shorty and Bernard, now standing eyeball to eyeball, give each other the once over, and they don't like what they see.

Shorty is the first to speak, "I could kick your ass."

Bernard replies, "You talking to me?"

"Yeah, I'm talking to you."

Bernard replies with an ultra-tough DeNiro voice. "You talkin' to me?"

"That's right, you little sawed-off half-pint piece of shit."

Bernard rolls his shoulders, "You talkin' to me?"

At this point, Rocky enters this pathetic display of trash-talkin'. "I could kick both your asses . . . at the same time."

Shorty doesn't seem to like Rocky any better than Bernard. "It looks to me like you're just another politician without balls."

Rocky cackles, "Maybe that's why I like kicking 'em."

Whereupon Rocky gives Shorty a kick in the groin, which doubles him up–and makes Bernard laugh.

Whereupon, as a penalty for laughing, Shorty gives Bernard a sock in the nose, sending him reeling into Rocky's crotch and knocking her over the rail and off the porch.

Which, in turn, sends her into a scampering rage to return to the battle scene and deliver a vicious kick into Bernard's balls.

Whereupon, Shorty lofts a flying kick directly into Rocky's groin. This only makes her laugh, before proceeding to give both Shorty and Bernard another vicious kick in the balls.

Whereupon, Hoppy, incited by the fearful beating his best friend is taking, charges Rocky. "Run, Bernard!" Grabbing Rocky by the hair just as she is about to send yet another kick into what is left of Bernard's balls, he yanks her to the ground.

Whereupon, Lulabell, outraged by the assault on her sister, attacks Hoppy. "Don't you dare abuse my little sister!"

And, as the free-for-all continues, Beauregard tilts his head back, looks up to the heavens, and begs a question, "What is the matter with these people?"

CHAPTER EIGHTEEN

Meanwhile, back in Reno, an evening news report comes onto the local television screens, and an anchorman delivers the nightly news.

"Global war number 177 broke out today when the Republic of Glistening Rainbows, a small island in the South Pacific, attacked the Republic of Cascading Rivers. Initial reports suggested minor injuries to both sides. However, in a bulletin received just moments ago, it has now been confirmed that the entire population of both islands was lost when a bomb went off accidentally as it was being rowed into battle.

"On a lighter note, the funniest murder of the day took place in Pleasantville, Oregon, when an unemployed lumberjack returned from a fishing trip and caught his wife in bed with a member of the Sierra Club."

The anchorman continues with a chuckle, "An autopsy revealed the victim had been beaten to death with a trout. Good God Almighty, what's next."

UPCOMING BOOKS FROM THE *"12 STORIES FROM THE CAMPFIRES OF MY MIND"* SERIES BY DAVID CREPS

1
KING BOSS

Even if you are naturally inclined to shrug off life's constant parade of disappointments by simply denying their ultimate relevance, what's your method for disregarding a doctor's assurance that you will be dead within a month? For Johnny James, the King Boss, it meant he had one last chance to live. Finally.

2
SWANKY SHAMPANE

This comedy set in Reno, Beverly Hills, and Malibu is the story of Best Actress nominee, Swanky Shampane, a two-timing, double-dealing, poetically-profane, ridiculously-neurotic, but fabulously charming, former cat house prostitute, obsessed with changing her public image prior to the night of the Academy Awards when she will be taking the front-row-center-seat next to her bitterest rival, "that filthy bitch" . . . Myrtle Street.

3
THE NEW YEARS RESOLUTION

A romantic comedy concerning the last two people a merciful God would ever put together under one roof, especially during the week that one of them is giving up cigarettes.

It's what happens when ridiculously neurotic egos do battle while under the pressures of a calm biological attraction.

4
THE OTHER BROTHERS

A Disney-style comedy about two twelve-year-old boys. One black. One white. One from the mean streets of Harlem, one from an isolated chicken farm in Nevada.

Both too young to be full-fledged con artists, but both already in abundant possession of the devilish charm and swagger necessary for the calling should their lives continue along their current paths.

And were it not for their love of basketball and their mutual respect for the way each other plays the game, these two big-talkers might never have made it to the brotherhood that bonds them into a lifetime of friendship.

5
MARGARITAVILLE

Is the story of two bungling con artists living on a pathetic excuse for a sailboat, in a trailer park, while looking for that one big score that will get them to the warm, turquoise waters and sandy, white beaches of the Caribbean, where they can live "just like Jimmy Buffet."

6
THE ROAD TO JACK'S HOUSE

The story of a thirty-six-year-old virgin who has a very assertive opinion on every matter under the sun. And the guy who, at the time of meeting this woman, is engaged in a search for the answer to the question, "What is the best way for me to live the rest of my life?"

They are both a little pissy, both a little self-righteous, and they each have their own personal agendas when they head down Highway 395 to take her screenplay to Hollywood, where she has good reason to believe that it will be read by Jack Nicholson. At his house. On a Saturday afternoon–while she is swimming in his pool, during a star-studded, rollicking-romp of a barbeque.

7
LAST CHANCE

A chilling comedy about the possibilities of "what if?"

What if the focus of present-day science were trained on finding a way to eliminate all violent tendencies from human behavior?

And what if a relatively small group of well-funded scientists undertook this problem, in secret, and through genetic engineering were successful in solving it?

And what if they not only discovered the formula for making humanity a passive species, but at the same time realized a way to dispense this formula throughout the world—without notice and without permission? Should they?

(Now available on *Amazon*)

8
THE GREATEST MOVIE EVER WRITTEN

The attempt by an artist of questionable sanity to write and direct a movie that will literally "save the world." The pressure is great. The time is short. And by every initial indication, his thinking is way too far "outside the box."

Yet he perseveres, fueled by a single belief: "You can't prevent the human race from destroying itself with a bigger, better weapon. But if your thoughts are crazy enough . . . you might be able to do it with an idea."

9
THE REUNION

The story of what happens when a thirty-year class reunion brings together five old high school friends who have been suffering from the same secret guilt from so many years ago.

It is also the story of what happens when Elizabeth Maryann Walker spends her weekend with these same five guys, up in the mountains, camping at Bennies Creek, falling in love for the second time in her life–with the same man.

10
THE IRONY OF IT ALL

A story of what might have happened during the last few weeks of the 2000 presidential election if the writer, Chesterfield Johnson, a man of unusual perceptions and bizarre solutions, had convinced candidate Al Gore to act in accordance with Chesterfield's unsolicited advice.

Besides his strategy to win Mr. Gore the election, Chesterfield has also devised a strategy to get his latest screenplay into the hands of an aging actress desperate to find a script worthy of her talent.

And within these dual tracks of Chesterfield's efforts, live an assortment of schemers and manipulators operating in the guise of Hollywood agents, political insiders, tabloid celebrities, and talk show hosts.

11
ON THE WALL IN THE CAVE

This comedy explores the absurdities of what can happen when a seemingly normal American man goes into a cave in the mountains to meditate on the problems of the world with the intention of figuring out the solution to the whole mess.

Current news headlines from any part of the world make this character's mindset very easy to understand.

12
THE SWEET REDEMPTION OF REPREHENSIBLE BOB

This is the story of a reprehensible human being with an insatiable need to fondle breasts at every possibility. With or without permission.

And the lovely woman who had suffered enormously for twenty years, before deciding to track him down and "shoot him through the eyeballs."

(Now available on *Amazon*)

ABOUT DAVID CREPS

David has worked as a ditch-digger, truck driver, dice-dealer, carpenter, screenwriter, playwright, and novelist.

The first highlight of his writing career happened when he was twenty-two years old, and Shecky Greene read a couple pages of his stuff, and said, "I've read worse."

And, in analyzing the unspoken words within Shecky's comment, David understood Shecky to mean, "Holy crap! I am the greatest writer Shecky has ever allowed to work for him for free!"

This was enough to inspire him through decades of laborious scribbling and ultimately provide him with enough cash to get a small mortgage on a cabin 8,000 feet up in the mountains, and to purchase a genuine 1966 greenish-gray (a color occasionally referred to, behind his back, as puke-green) U.S. Postal Service mail truck lined with wall-to-wall-to-ceiling-to-floor green shag carpet, which could transport more lengths of lumber in one haul than any vehicle in this entire country.

(David is also a husband, a father, a brother, a grandfather, a good-natured, and occasionally, totally innocent, rascal.)